BETWEEN NOW AND ALWAYS

AWAL GANDHI

For a story that knew its way to my heart—long

before I knew how to write it.

For a name I never thought would turn

into a habit.

And for the feeling I'll always be slightly biased

about—between now and always.

For late-night drives, quiet smiles, and almost confessions.

Jhol – Maanu & Annural Khalid

Afsos – Anuv Jain & AP Dhillon

Until I Found You – Stephen Sanchez

Dooron Dooron – Paresh Pahuja, Shiv Tandan & Meghdeep

It's You – Ali Gatie

Perfect – Ed Sheeran

Paro – Aditya Rikhari & UNPLG'd

Say You Won't Let Go – James Arthur

I Guess I'm In Love – Clinton Kane

Humdum – Vishal Mishra

Author's Note

So... I finally did it.

This book happened.

Not because I had it all figured out—but because sometimes, stories just find you. In the quiet moments. In stolen glances. In the songs you overplay without even realising why.

Between Now and Always was written on ordinary days with an extraordinary feeling in my heart – the kind that makes you smile for no reason... or stare at your phone wondering if they're thinking of you too.

It's not some complicated love story.

It's simple. Soft. Maybe even a little silly in places.

But it's mine. And now—it's yours too.

If this book made you smile, made you think of *your someone*, or made you believe in soft love again—then I'm happier than words can say.

Thank you for picking up my first book—from my little world to yours.

I'll be back soon—probably still overthinking, still listening to love songs on a loop, and still writing stories that feel a little too personal.

With love,

Awal Gandhi

(currently daydreaming and calling it 'plot development')

Contents

1

Anaya

The voice of the music playing in the car speakers filled the silence between us. The only thing I was doing was looking out of the window with the biggest question in my mind, '**Why is he taking me out for a random drive all of a sudden?**'. My fingers were fidgeting with the edge of my hoodie, the weight of all my thoughts heavy against my chest.

"You're very quiet tonight," he finally spoke, glancing at me with a half smile across his face.

Flirty? Friendly? Mocking? Guess I'll never be able to figure out what that smile meant.

"You called me for a drive at ten pm all of a sudden. What am I supposed to say?" I replied.

He laughed softly. *Cute.* I mused briefly before shaking off the idea.

The last time we were alone like this was around five years ago when he was dropping me home after some class we had together. That was the time I had a serious crush on him which I thought I had outgrown. Turns out, I was wrong. Now he was here - more handsome, mature, warmer, but I just couldn't tell if all of it was real or if my imagination was playing tricks on me.

"So, what is this drive about?" I finally spoke.

"Just felt like seeing you!" he shrugged.

My heart stuttered. What was I supposed to do with that?

The background music was the only sound between us for a while; his words, 'Just felt like seeing you', were doing cartwheels in my stomach. That wasn't something a friend would say, right?

I stole a glance at him. His perfect eyes were glued to the road, but his jaw was tensed, which suggested that he was not as calm as he was pretending to be.

"So........" I hesitated, "you just felt like driving around?"

He glanced at me for a brief second and then returned his eyes to the road. "Yeah." His lips curled into the same half smile as before. "I figured we could catch up."

Catch up? I hadn't seen him since the last time I was out with my friends, where he also happened to hang out, and we awkwardly exchanged a side hug around a year ago. There were a few casual texts here and there, but never the ones that felt like an actual conversation. But now? There was the same familiarity but something felt new, *different.*

"Okay," I tried to sound as casual as I could. "What's up with you lately?"

"Same old me, going to work and trying not to get in trouble," he said.

"Trying, huh?" I asked.

"Yeah, You know how I am," he smirked.

Then after a couple of minutes, he sighed and added, "I don't know, I thought it would be good to do something….spontaneous."

I chuckled, "Spontaneous? A random drive at night?"

He glanced at me, his eyes lingering a little longer than before. "I guess it is nice to do some things without giving them a second thought."

There it was again - the feeling of something different. He had never talked to me like that. It was something I wasn't able to comprehend.

"What are we doing out here?" I asked.

"I don't know yet, but I guess we can figure it out," he smiled at me.

My heart skipped a beat, but I immediately regretted the thought - maybe I was reading too much into this.

He didn't behave like the same guy I knew back then, but maybe that was the point, and it was not just a drive.

2

Anaya

⚜

The drive ended way too quickly, but I could still hear the soft hum of the engine in my head as he parked his car outside my house.

"Thanks for the ride," I said, with a smile on my face that seemed more of a polite gesture than something genuine.

"Anytime," he nodded, his smile unreadable. It felt like he had something to say, which he didn't. I started heading back to my house.

"Anaya......."

I immediately froze when I heard my name from his mouth in a soft, serious tone instead of a stupid mocking nickname he had for me.

I turned around. "Yes?" The words had merely any voice in them.

"You remember you told me that you liked me back in school?" He asked.

I thought I would collapse under the weight of his gaze and the tone of his voice. I finally gathered some power to say, "Yeah, well…..that was a long time ago." "Things change," the words almost felt like a defence.

I could hear him move, a step closer. All I could see in front of me were flashbacks of me stealing secret glances at him and all the things I felt like telling him straight to his face but I didn't. I could feel him trying to study me.

He paused for a bit before asking, "Do you still like me?"

I could feel the ground beneath me slipping away. Do I? Well, I guess so, but I had no clue how I was supposed to answer his question. I wanted to answer him and tell him the truth, but the truth felt like a betrayal. I was not ready for heartbreak again.

I opened my mouth to speak, but no words came out. My heart was screaming one thing, but my head was too afraid to follow through.

The silence stretched between us. "It's late. I should head inside." I turned back and raced towards my house.

He called for me again, but by the time I turned back, I saw that he had gotten back in his car and driven away.

What did I just do? The quiet of the night seemed louder, the weight of his question echoing in my heart.

I didn't have an answer yet, but the more I thought about it, the harder it became to convince myself that maybe I didn't feel something. He was and is *my first love* and it just doesn't go away. Does it?

3

Kabir

I did not know where I was driving to. Just aimlessly driving around streets was something I did very often, but I never had thoughts in my mind. The things I was feeling back then were inexplicable.

I replayed the moment outside her house in my mind. What the hell was I thinking? *Do you still like me?* Who even asks that? And where was it coming from? I had no clue.

It just came out... like it was some truth hidden inside me like it was something I needed to know even without knowing what answer I would like.

Did I want her to say yes? Did I want her to say no? I just didn't know.

I found myself remembering the moment she admitted she had once liked me. I hadn't known, and when I asked what she meant and why she phrased it in the past tense, she just laughed uncomfortably and steered the conversation elsewhere as if it was nothing more than a passing thought.

Why was this fact confusing me now? Why could I not stop thinking about it?

She looked different that day - older, more guarded. And when she walked away, it felt like I was losing something I didn't even know I wanted to keep. Or maybe, I was just overthinking it. Maybe this was wrong.

God! So confusing!

The drive was meant to be nothing more than a few hours on the road. But sometimes, the simplest moments have a way of changing everything.

I just wanted to see her and catch up like old friends do. Why the hell did I have to remember the sudden bomb she dropped on me? Did I feel something for her? I didn't know.

And that was the worst part. What if I messed up everything by asking her that stupid question?

I pulled over to the side of the road, my chest tight with frustration. My thoughts were running in circles, and I couldn't make sense of any of them. She was my friend, well at least that's what I thought. Back in school, we mostly just talked about studies. I was never really close to her, but there was always this easy familiarity between us.

All I knew was that the way she looked at me and fumbled did something to me, but I wasn't sure if I was ready to figure out what it meant.

Was I supposed to pretend it never happened? Act like we were just two friends catching up?

But if it was true, why did I feel like a part of me was going away when she turned back? I didn't know what it meant, and that terrified me.

4

Anaya

⸻ ❧ ⸻

It took me four years to get over him, and now, the feelings are resurfacing. I do not have the emotional energy to go through it all again - liking him, hoping something would happen, and then being left with nothing. Either he is all mine, or we never see each other again.

At least, that's what I promised myself.

But the moment my phone's screen lit up with a notification from him asking if I wanted to grab a coffee, my resolve crumbled. Before I could think twice, I replied, "Sure, what time?"

Why do you do this to yourself, Anaya?

I had to go with him around six, but the anxiety started hitting me around four. My mind was a mess of questions. Would it be awkward to face him? What would we talk about? And… what would I wear? Wait, what? Since when did I care about my outfits?

Somehow, I managed to pull myself together and get ready. At exactly six, he called.

"I'm outside," he said.

I grabbed my bag, took a deep breath, and headed outside. He greeted me with a side hug - warm, familiar, and maddeningly confusing. He smiled.

"Take the wheel today."

The drive started with polite small talk.

"How are you?" he asked.

"I'm good! What about you? How was your day?"

"The day was fine, and I believe the evening will be better," he shrugged.

My grip on the steering wheel tightened as heat flooded my cheeks. Stop, Kabir. Stop saying things like that.

We drove through a fast-food point, and he insisted on getting fries and chicken. I waited for him to hand me over the food, but instead, he held out a fry and fed me with his own hands, like it was the most natural thing in the world.

"What are you doing?" I asked, flustered.

"You're driving. I don't want you to crash," he said with a mischievous grin.

I rolled my eyes but opened my mouth. His eyes lingered on me, and I swear my heart nearly jumped to my mouth.

And then, as if things weren't already overwhelming, he listened to every bit of my nonsensical rambling during the drive. No interruptions, no roasting - just pure attention, like I was saying the most interesting things in the world.

I glanced at him when we stopped at the red light. He was already looking at me and it was as if his gaze was pulling secrets out of me.

By the time the drive ended, I was emotionally drained in the best way possible. He hugged me goodbye - a lingering hug that left me breathless.

Neither of us mentioned what had happened the previous night, but the way he acted today made one thing clear: Kabir wasn't just a crush. *I probably loved him.*

5

Anaya

My mind was replaying the moments from the previous evening - the way he was feeding me, the way he was listening to my nonsense, and most of all, the way he was looking at me as if he saw something he hadn't noticed before. It was so frustrating.

I couldn't concentrate on anything. I had sat down to read a book, then scrolled mindlessly on my phone, and even thought about organising my closet, but nothing could drown out the swirl of my thoughts. His voice, his gaze - haunted me.

What was happening? Was he just being kind? Or was it something deeper?

I wanted clarity but confronting him felt like a risk. What if I asked him and ruined whatever was building between us?

For once, I wanted to feel what it felt like to be admired by him.

My phone buzzed, interrupting my thoughts.

Kabir: "Hey! Up for a drive?"

Maybe this was my chance to understand what actually was happening.

Anaya: "Sure! Pick me up in 30?"

I hurried to get ready, nerves fluttering in my stomach. When I stepped out of my house, there he was, leaning casually against his car. But something was off - a figure sat in the passenger seat.

I blinked, confused.

"Hey!" Kabir greeted with a familiar smile. "I brought someone along."

The passenger door swung open, and Aarav, an old friend from school, stepped out with a wide grin.

"Surprise!" he laughed. "Kabir said we were going for a drive!"

Plastering on a polite smile, I climbed in the backseat. My heart sank. This wasn't the moment I imagined.

The drive started with loud laughs and school anecdotes. Kabir was charming, playful, and completely at ease - like Kabir from school, not the one who had looked at me with such intensity just the other night.

"You remember Anaya's legendary chemistry lab meltdown?" Aarav said between laughs.

Kabir smirked, his eyes glinting with mischief. "You mean when she got locked inside and cried over her incomplete titration?"

I froze. "Wait - how do you know that?"

He glanced at me through the mirror. "You told me back in school, remember?"

"No, I didn't."

He grinned. "I have my sources."

Aarav chuckled, "Dude, she was fuming when she came out."

"And you two are enjoying it now?" I snapped, trying to sound annoyed.

Kabir shrugged. "It's a classic Anaya story."

Their teasing should've annoyed me, but I found myself laughing along. Yet, something felt off.

This Kabir wasn't the same person from last night. He was light-hearted and friendly - like a version of him that belonged to the past.

Had I imagined the connection between us?

When Aarav finally got off at his house, Kabir turned to me with a casual smile.

"Fun, right?" he asked.

I forced a smile. "Yes, definitely!"

But inside, I was anything but okay.

When we reached outside my house, he waved me goodbye. As I was heading inside my house, one thought ran in my mind:

I was done analysing his moves.

If Kabir had something to say, he would have to say it outright. I wasn't confessing my feelings this time.

I'd let things unfold naturally - but this time, I wasn't chasing answers.

6

Kabir

The drive with Aarav and Anaya had been strange. It was like I was slipping back into old habits—mocking her, teasing her, acting like we were just old friends from school. But when I saw the way she reacted, the polite smile she forced, something inside me felt... off. It didn't sit right.

I kept replaying the moments from the drive in my mind. The easy banter with Aarav, the casual way I treated her, but it wasn't like before. Something had shifted between us, and I didn't know how to fix it.

When I had driven Anaya alone the other night, everything felt natural—her presence, her smile, even her rambling about nothing. I actually enjoyed it. Hell, I found myself looking forward to seeing her again. But tonight? Tonight, I was cold. *Detached.*

What was I doing?

I knew what it felt like when things were simple between us - back in school, when I didn't feel this weird tug of something else, something I didn't want to acknowledge. But now? Every time I saw her, it felt like a spark was waiting to ignite.

And I hated it.

The worst part? I was confusing myself. I didn't know if I was supposed to be the old friend, the one who teased her endlessly, or the guy who'd shared a quiet drive with her, the one who saw something in her eyes that made my chest feel tight.

Why the hell was I so afraid to admit that maybe... just maybe... I liked her more than I was letting on?

I groaned, slamming my hand against the steering wheel. Why couldn't I just figure this out? Why couldn't I just ask her how she felt instead of pretending everything was fine when it wasn't??

I hadn't told anyone, but the truth was, I was scared. Scared that I'd mess things up. Scared that if I admitted how I felt, I'd lose her forever.

When I asked her that stupid question the other night—Do you still like me?—I had no idea what I wanted to hear. Part of me longed for her to say no, to confirm that I wasn't crazy for feeling like this. But another part of me wanted her to say yes, just so I could finally let go of all the doubt.

But she dodged it. She walked away without answering.

Maybe she wasn't sure either.

But what now?

I hated this confusion. It wasn't like me to be uncertain. I'd always known what I wanted. But with Anaya, everything was different.

It felt like I was standing at the edge of something, but I couldn't bring myself to jump.

The drive with her had been simple—no extra meaning, no baggage. But now? I didn't know how to look at her without wondering if it meant something more.

And if it did, what would I do?

I had to figure it out. I had to stop pretending nothing was happening. But for now, I needed space to clear my head. I was done letting the confusion control me.

I wasn't going to make any decisions yet. Not until I understood what was going on in my damn head.

But if I were being honest, a part of me was terrified of what might happen if I figured it out.

7

Kabir

◆◆

Another evening, another drive. It was not meant to be anything unusual. A few minutes of mindless chatter, her rambling about something that I secretly enjoy, and then dropping her off. Simple.

Except this time, when I pulled up outside her house, Things didn't go as planned.

Just as Anaya was about to leave, another car pulled behind mine. *Her father.*

I had seen him in passing, but we had never spoken. And even before I could think of leaving, he waved at me and gestured for me to enter. I glanced at Anaya, expecting her to say something, but she only gave me an amused look- like she was waiting to see how I reacted.

So, I stepped outside the car.

We sat in the living room. I had spoken to hundreds of people before—clients, professors, suppliers—but sitting across from her father felt different. He asked me about my work and my family, and I answered everything smoothly, but it felt like I was being examined.

Anaya sat there the whole time, mostly quiet, occasionally jumping in with comments that made her dad smile. Meanwhile, I couldn't decide whether to relax or stay on my best behaviour.

Fifteen minutes. That's it. Eventually, I stood up to leave, and as I stepped outside the door, Anaya walked with me. Just as I was about to step into my car, she smiled and waved at me, her gaze holding onto me a moment longer than usual.

I drove off, but my mind was still there - sitting in the living room, replaying all that I had said. Did I sound polite enough? Did I talk too much? Not enough? Why did I care?

The next thing I knew, I pulled out my phone and dialled Anaya.

"Did I talk properly?"

A pause. "What?"

"With Uncle. Did I behave properly?"

A beat of silence and then a short laugh. "Kabir, are you seriously overthinking this?"

"Just answer yes or no," I said too quickly.

She chuckled but something about her voice was softer when she finally said, "Yes. You did."

I muttered a quick "Okay" and hung up before she could say anything else.

The moment the call ended, I frowned at my phone. What was I doing? This wasn't me. I never second-guessed myself and never cared about what anyone thought. But tonight, something felt off.

And I had no idea why.

8

Anaya

I stared at my screen long after the call ended. A slow smile crept onto my face. He really called just to ask if he behaved properly in front of dad? Kabir - the ever-confident, never second-guessing anything Kabir? Overthinking about this?

Interesting. Very interesting. The next time we meet, I knew exactly what to do.

*****

We were sitting in the car with our half-finished cups of coffee in our hands. He was talking about something random, but I was not listening. I was too busy planning my attack.

When he paused, I leaned back in my seat, stretching my arms. "By the way," I said casually, "Dad said something interesting about you after you left."

His head snapped towards me so fast I almost laughed out loud. "What?"

I took a slow sip of my coffee, enjoying how his brows furrowed in confusion. If I could only bottle up this moment - Kabir, the unreadable Kabir, hanging on to my very word.

"What did he say?" He pressed, eyes narrowing.

"I don't know if I should tell you," I shrugged.

His jaw tightened. "Anaya."

I half bit my lip, trying not to laugh. "I mean… he seems really interested in you."

"What does that even mean?"

I gasped dramatically. "You're getting nervous. This is adorable."

He scoffed, his cheeks turned to the faintest shade of pink. "I'm not nervous. Just tell me."

I pretended to think for a moment. "He said you seem… different."

Kabir leaned in slightly, his curiosity outweighing his usual patience. "Different, how?"

I exhaled, pretending to weigh my words carefully, "Like, more aware of something."

His forehead creased, "Wait, what? What did he mean?"

I tilted my head. "I don't know. You tell me."

He shook his head. "You're impossible."

I let out a laugh, finally dropping my act. "Relax. He just said you seemed like a nice guy. That's all."

His shoulders relaxed, and for a second, I thought that was the end of it. But then he looked straight into my eyes, something unreadable in his gaze. "Do you feel the same?"

The question caught me off guard. My throat went dry.

I wasn't sure how to answer the question without revealing too much, so I smirked and said, "You? Nice? That's still up for debate."

He chuckled, shaking his head as he returned to his coffee. But his expression was different like he was thinking about something he wouldn't say out loud.

I was just tired of constantly trying to make sense of him.

9

Anaya

Days passed, and Kabir and I kept meeting every now and then. Nothing drastic had changed the weight of an unsettled conversation still hanging between us. But I had bigger things to focus on.

A few days later, I got the news.

I got placed at Deloitte.

I kept staring at the email, trying to process the words I had just read. Was it for real? I pinched myself.

No, I was not dreaming. It was really happening.

After telling my parents and sinking in their happiness, my first instinct was to call Kabir.

He picked up almost instantly. "What's up?"

I took a deep breath, trying to keep my excitement in check. "I have news."

"Good news or bad news?"

"Very good news."

"Okay, tell me already," he said, sounding amused.

"I got placed at Deloitte."

There was a beat of silence. Then, "Anaya, that's great! I am so proud of you."

The warmth in his voice made me smile even wider. "Thanks! I was thinking... I owe you a treat for tolerating me all these years. How about dinner tomorrow?"

"I'm never saying no to free food," he teased. "Done."

*****

The next evening, we met at a cafe - not too crowded or fancy, just how we liked it. The energy between us was light and easy, filled with playful banter and laughter. For once, no complicated emotions were lurking in the background.

Everything was good until it wasn't.

At some point during dinner, he asked, "So… when do you start?"

"Next month," I replied.

"That's soon."

"Yeah. I'll have to shift to Hyderabad."

The change was immediate.

His grip on the fork tightened. He tried to keep his expression neutral, but I noticed the shift in his eyes. Something had clicked into place - something he wasn't sure he liked.

For the first time that evening, he was quiet.

"Are you okay?" I asked, tilting my head.

He blinked, snapping out of his thoughts. "Yeah, of course," he forced a smile, but I wasn't convinced.

I knew him too well.

Something about this had unsettled him. I just didn't know what.

And maybe... neither did he.

10

Kabir

———— ✦✦ ————

Anaya and I hadn't met in days. She was busy packing, running errands, and collecting things for her move. But she had promised that we'd meet before she left.

We still texted, though. Stupid, meaningless conversations.

She had sent me a snap of a half-packed suitcase with "How do people even do this?"

I replied "Just shove the stuff inside and sit on it."

She sent a laughing emoji. "I tried. Didn't work."

It was normal. We were normal. But then, why was I stuck on that night?

I leaned back in my chair, staring at the phone. The factory was quieter than usual, maybe just because I wasn't listening. I had been distracted when she said she was moving to Hyderabad.

I should've expected it. She was always ambitious - of course, she would get a great job. It wasn't like she was leaving forever. We'd still talk and meet when she came back.

Then why did I feel like something was slipping away?

I hadn't even realised I had zoned out that night until she asked me if I was okay. And I lied. Just forced a smile and moved past it.

But the truth was, I didn't know why I froze. And I hated that.

I wasn't the kind of guy who sat around emotions. But now, my mind was tangled with thoughts I didn't want to acknowledge.

Why did it matter this much?

Why did I feel like I was running out of time?

I exhaled sharply, pushing my phone aside. Maybe I was overthinking. Maybe once she left, things would settle in my mind. Or maybe… I needed to figure this out before it was too late.

Before I knew it, I was dialling Aarav.

He picked up. "To what do I owe the honour?"

I ignored his sarcasm. "Where are you?"

"At work. Why?"

"Meet me today. I need to talk."

A knowing sigh. "It's about Anaya. Isn't it?"

I scowled. "Just meet me."

*****

Four hours later, Aarav strolled into my room like he had all the time in the world. "Alright. Spill."

"She's leaving in two days."

"I know." He sat on the chair. "And?"

"And…" I exhaled. "I don't know. I feel-"

I stopped, rubbing my hand on my face. "Forget it."

Aarav tilted his head, studying me like a puzzle he was about to solve. "You feel weird about it."

I didn't answer. He leaned forward. "You don't understand why it is bothering you so much."

I shot him a look. "Are you enjoying this?"

"A little," he admitted. "But mostly, I am waiting for you to get a clue."

I sighed. "It's just - why did I freeze when she said it? Why did my brain go completely blank?"

Aarav smirked. "Because, my friend, you're an idiot."

I glared at him.

He continued. "You've spent all this time thinking nothing has changed like she's the same Anaya you knew in school. But the second Hyderabad came into the picture, it hit you that she won't be around anymore."

I looked away.

Aarav leaned back. "You don't have to say it out loud, but at least be honest with yourself. If you don't figure out what she means to you now, you might never get a chance again."

That stuck.

Anaya had promised we'd meet, so I had one last drive left with her before everything changed.

And for the first time in a long time, I didn't know if I was ready for it.

11

Kabir

The night air felt cool, carrying the faint scent of rain, but I barely noticed. Anaya sat across from me, sipping her usual cold coffee, rambling about something that had happened while she was packing.

She was laughing, eyes crinkling that familiar way, and I wasn't listening.

Or maybe I was, but not to her words.

I was listening to how her voice dipped when she was telling a joke, the way she absentmindedly played with her straw, and how her pitch went up when she was excited.

I had spent years thinking she was just Anaya - my old friend, the girl who had always been there, the person who never made me feel I was dumb because I asked something too basic.

But she wasn't just Anaya anymore. And that realisation sat heavy in my chest.

"Are you even paying attention?" Her voice cut through my thoughts.

I blinked. "Huh?"

She narrowed her eyes. "You totally zoned out."

"I did not."

She smirked. "Yeah? What was I talking about?"

I opened my mouth and then closed it.

She grinned. "That's what I thought."

I rolled my eyes, trying to shake off whatever was going on inside me. "You talk too much. It's hard to keep up."

She gasped in the fake offence. "Wow. So now I'm annoying?"

"I did not say that."

"But you implied it." She crossed her arms. "And I was about to give you a heartfelt goodbye."

Something in my chest tightened at that word. *Goodbye.*

This was our last night before she left. I wanted to say something - anything that would make sense of what I was feeling. But every time I opened my mouth, the words got stuck.

So, I did what I always did. I covered it up.

"You're being dramatic," I said, leaning back in my chair. "And I don't do sentimental goodbyes."

She tilted her head, studying me. "So, what do you do?"

He shrugged. "Just…..see you later."

She exhaled, shaking her head with a small smile. "Fine. See you later, Kabir."

But something in her expression told me she knew I wasn't saying everything I wanted to. And something in mine told her that maybe I never would.

12

Anaya

The street was quieter than usual. The soft glow of streetlights cast shadows inside the car, highlighting the edges of his face - the same face I had memorised over the years, the face that now somehow felt… different.

He tapped his fingers on the steering wheel. I curled mine around my phone. Neither of us moved to open the door.

"Well," he exhaled, "This is it."

I nodded, but my throat was too tight to say anything.

A few more seconds of silence stretched between us before he finally unbuckled his seatbelt and stepped out of the car. I followed, my heart pounding for reasons I refused to acknowledge.

When I turned to say goodbye, he was already looking at me. Not in his usual, unreadable way, but as if he wanted to say something - but just couldn't.

Instead, he opened his arms slightly, almost hesitant. A goodbye hug.

I stepped forward and wrapped my arms around him.

And that's when I realised just how tall he was.

Kabir stood at six feet, while I barely reached 5'4. My head naturally rested against his chest, and before I could stop myself, I noticed the steady rhythm of his heartbeat. Strong. Even. But... was it my imagination, or did it pick up speed for a second?

He tightened his grip around me.

Neither of us spoke.

Neither of us let go.

We just stood there, caught in something unspoken, something I wasn't ready to name.

Not yet.

13

Kabir

It had been days since Anaya left, but something about her absence felt… heavier than it should have.

We still texted on and off, but the rhythm felt different - slower, offbeat. I told myself that it was because she was busy settling in, but deep down, I knew that wasn't it. The problem wasn't her. It was me.

She sent me something funny late at night. I even smiled, but I didn't reply, and I have no clue why. It was like my brain was actively stopping me from replying the way I usually would.

And then came the call. "Why do you sound weird?" she had noticed.

"I don't," I said too quickly.

"Liar."

I chuckled and tried to sound normal. "You're in Hyderabad, Anaya. The network there is making me sound weird."

"Oh, please."

Normally, I'd tease her back, dragging the conversation into something ridiculous. But today, I did not have that in me. Because the truth was, I didn't know what was wrong with me.

Then she brought up the hug.

"You didn't say anything about our very emotional and dramatic goodbye, Kabir," she said with a playful voice, but I knew there was something behind it.

I exhaled, rubbing my temple. "It was a hug, Anaya."

"A long hug," she corrected, "A tight hug."

I could almost see her smirk, but my chest felt heavy for some reason. It had been a long hug. And I did not want to let go.

"Do you miss me already?" she teased.

I laughed, "Are you fishing for compliments now?"

She huffed. "You're impossible."

I should've said something then. I should've told her that things felt different now. I wasn't sure why I zoned out when she mentioned that she was leaving. That I still hadn't fully processed what it meant.

Instead, I let the silence stretch between us.

And then, out of nowhere, she asked, "Kabir, are you okay?"

I didn't reply. Not because I didn't want to, but because I wasn't sure of the answer.

14

Anaya

———— ✦✦ ————

I stared at the ceiling, waiting.

It wasn't like Kabir to go quiet like this.

Sure, he took his time replying sometimes, but this was different. I had asked if something was wrong, and he had gone completely silent. That was new.

"…Kabir?" I prompted, shifting the phone against my ear.

Still nothing.

I frowned. "Hello? Did the network drop, or are you just ignoring me?"

"I'm here," he said.

"Okay… then are you going to answer my question?"

The conversation had a hitch, the kind that only happens when someone is deciding what to say next.

"Anaya, you think too much." He exhaled a small laugh, but it was not the usual amused one.

"Oh, I overthink? You're the one acting weird." I narrowed my eyes.

"I'm not acting weird."

I huffed. "Fine, if you say so."

"Anyway," I said after a moment, forcing a lighter tone, "at least pretend to miss me."

This time, his laugh was real. "Do you want me to beg you to come back or what?"

I smirked, "Maybe."

"You should settle in first."

Well, this was not the reply I was expecting.

Before I could press further, I heard a knock on my door.

"Anaya, dinner!" My roommate's voice rang from the other side.

Right. Zoya.

"Ugh, I gotta go," I muttered into the phone, "But Kabir?"

"Hmm?"

"You're acting weird."

He didn't respond. Not immediately. But just as I was about to say something else, his voice came through - low, careful.

"I'll talk to you later, Anaya."

And just like that, he cut the call. I stared at my phone for a while before groaning and getting up.

*****

I met Zoya on my first day here. She was the kind of person who could turn a room lively within seconds—confident, sharp, and witty—but too observant for my own good.

When I got to the dining table, she was already having her sandwich, scrolling through her phone.

"What's with the long face?" she asked as soon as she saw me.

"Nothing," I replied, rubbing my face.

"See? That is why I don't trust people who say 'nothing' because it always means 'everything'.

I scoffed but didn't respond.

A few minutes passed in silence before she finally spoke again. "Wait… Does it have to do something with the guy to whom you were talking just now?"

I froze mid-bite.

"Oh my God," she gasped. "It is about him. Who is he? Your boyfriend? Ex? Childhood love?"

I rolled my eyes. "None of the above."

Her grin widened. "Then tell me."

I hesitated. Talking about Kabir felt big. But Zoya was looking at me expectantly, and honestly? I needed to get it out of my system.

So, I told her. About Kabir, about our history, about the way he confused the hell out of me.

By the time I was done, she was so engrossed that her half-eaten sandwich sat untouched.

"So let me get this straight," she said finally, tilting her head. "You had feelings for him before and you still probably do. And he's acting all weird about it but not saying anything?"

"Pretty much."

She folded her arms. "Girl, that man is scared."

I blinked. "What?"

"He's panicking. He probably just realised something, and he doesn't know what to do about the realisation."

I exhaled. "Okay. But what do I do about it?"

Zoya grinned. "Easy. Call him on it."

"What do you mean?"

"You don't have to confess or anything, but at least you can push him to acknowledge whatever weird energy he is giving off. Next time you talk, just mention it. Casually. See how he reacts."

I thought about it. It wasn't a bad idea. I had spent enough time overanalysing his moves. Maybe it was time to stop waiting.

I picked up my phone and dialled his number.

"You're calling again?" His voice was lighter this time, teasing. But I wasn't backing off.

"So Kabir," I said, leaning back in my chair. "Are you planning to keep acting strange, or are we finally going to talk about it?"

A long pause.

Zoya grinned from across the table. "Oh, this is gonna be fun."

And honestly, I agreed.

15

Kabir

Absolutely no words were coming out of my mouth, no matter how much I tried.

I have been preparing for this. Rehearsing. But when she was right there at the other end of the call, I just couldn't get myself to speak.

"Are you still there?" Anaya's voice broke through my thoughts, soft but laced with confusion.

I shut my eyes and took a breath. Just say it.

"I-yeah. I'm here," I exhaled, "I just-"

The silence stretched between us, and for a second, I thought Anaya would say something to fill it, but she didn't. She was waiting.

"Anaya, I-" my voice faltered even before the words came out.

I wanted to tell her that yes, I had led her on. I had felt that shift, the change, that thing between us that neither of us had spoken about.

But I also wanted to tell her that I needed time. I wanted to be sure. It was not something I could take lightly. The last thing I wanted was to hurt her.

Somehow, I managed to force the words out of my mouth. "I just…..needed to figure things out."

A pause. "Figure out what?"

I swallowed. "Us."

She spoke after a while, her voice softer than before. "What do you mean?"

I exhaled, sharply. "I mean - I felt something, Anaya. That night, when I hugged you and even before that. I knew you noticed it, too."

Another pause. Too long.

Then, she let out a soft laugh. But it wasn't the kind that would make me laugh along. It was hollow. Doubtful.

"You're confusing me, Kabir."

I felt something tighten in my chest. That was the last thing I wanted.

"I know," I admitted, "And I'm sorry. I-I just don't want to say anything until I'm sure of it. Because if I say it, it is real. And if it is real, then I have to know I won't mess it up."

Another silence.

Then she sighed. "And when will you be sure?"

I shut my eyes. "Soon."

I heard her breathe out, and her voice was unreadable when she spoke up again. "Okay."

That was it.

Just okay.

There was no pushing, no questioning, just a simple acceptance. And somehow, it felt worse. If she wasn't pushing anymore… maybe it meant she was done waiting.

16

Anaya

For a few seconds after the call ended, I stared at my phone. Did that actually happen? Did Kabir actually say that?

He led me on. That's what he admitted, right? But not because he was playing around - but because he needed time. *Time to be sure.*

My heart raced. My fingers curled around my phone, itching to call him back, to push him for answers. But I didn't because I wasn't scared of the answer anymore.

I had spent years thinking if Kabir could ever see me that way. If he could ever feel the way I felt about him. And now, for the first time, it wasn't just me overthinking things. He was thinking about it too.

It wasn't a yes. But it wasn't a no either.

A smile crept onto my face. For the longest time, I had imagined what it would be like to date Kabir. To be someone he chose to be with. And now maybe - just maybe - it was possible.

But there was also a risk. Because if he was still figuring things out, there was a chance he could realise he didn't want this. That he could back off even before things began.

The thought made my stomach twist, but I shook it away. I had spent enough time waiting for him before. This time, I wouldn't do that.

A voice snapped me out of my thoughts.

"So? What happened?"

I saw Zoya sitting across from me, arms crossed, eyes practically beaming with curiosity.

"I-" I opened my mouth to explain, but no words came out. How was I even supposed to put this into words?

"You cut the call and immediately started grinning like an idiot, which means something happened."

I bit my lip, trying to suppress my smile. "He said… he led me on."

"Excuse me?" Her eyes widened.

"Not like that," I rushed to explain. "I mean he didn't do it on purpose. He just needed time to be sure."

Zoya stared at me for a second before blowing out a low whistle. "Damn, so he feels something but he is too much of a coward to admit it yet?"

"Something like that."

Zoya raised an eyebrow. "And? What are you going to do?"

I picked up my phone and stared at his contact poster, then locked it and set it aside.

"Nothing." I said firmly. "I'm not going to text or call him. If he really wants this, he'll reach out."

Zoya studied me for a moment before nodding approvingly. "Good. Make him sweat a little."

I laughed, shaking my head. "It's not about making him sweat."

"Yeah, yeah," she waved me off. "Just be ready for… anything. Okay?" I exhaled. Whatever happened next, I'd be ready for it.

17

Kabir

I lay on my bed, staring at the ceiling. What had I just done?

I had admitted it. Not entirely, not completely - but I had. And Anaya had caught on. She wasn't dumb. She knew there was something between us, and now, for the first time, I couldn't pretend it didn't exist.

But what now? Was I ready for this? Was I even allowed to want this?

A sigh escaped me as I shut my eyes, my mind still racing. I wanted to believe that I had time to figure it out. That Anaya wasn't going anywhere.

The thought stayed with me till exhaustion pulled me to sleep.

*****

It was a bright, sunny day. I was standing somewhere unfamiliar, surrounded by laughter and chatter. My eyes searched the space - for her.

And then I saw her. Anaya.

She was smiling - no, beaming - as she stood next to someone. Tall. Confident. Handsome.

Everything she ever wanted.

My stomach twisted. I wanted to move, to say something to her - but my feet wouldn't budge. I was stuck, forced to watch.

The guy leaned in, whispering something in her ear, and she laughed - really laughed - the kind of laugh that reached her eyes.

I had seen that laugh before. I had been the reason for it a hundred times.

But not this time. Not anymore.

My chest tightened as the guy wrapped an arm around her, pulling her close. She didn't hesitate. She leaned in like she belonged there. Like she was happy.

And then, as if sensing my presence, she turned her head. Our eyes met. I wanted to call out to her, say something, anything - but before I could, she looked away. Like I wasn't even there. Like I didn't matter anymore.

*****

I jolted awake, heart pounding, breath uneven.

It took me a second to realise where I was - that it was all just a dream.

But even as the reality kicked in, the panic didn't fade away. Because what if it wasn't just a dream?

What if I was waiting too long? What if by the time I figured things out, Anaya had already moved on?

What if I lost her - before I even had her?

18

Kabir

I sat in my car, gripping the steering wheel as if it were the only thing keeping me grounded. The dim glow of the streetlights barely reached inside, casting long, restless shadows across the dashboard.

I hadn't driven anywhere, just sitting in the car parked outside my house, staring blankly at the road ahead. My mind was still trapped in my dream, my heart still hammering as if it were real.

Because for those terrifying moments, it had been real. Anaya was with someone else. She looked happy—happier than I had ever seen her. The guy beside her was effortlessly charming and had the kind of confidence that made it clear he knew exactly what he wanted.

And what he wanted was *her.*

I had stood frozen, unable to move, unable to speak—just watching her as she laughed. She looked at him the way she used to look at me.

The moment I woke up from my dream, drenched in cold sweat, I hadn't even stopped to think. I just grabbed my keys and left. But running away hadn't helped. I was still there, still spiralling, still hearing her laugh from the dream as if it were mocking me.

I exhaled a sharp breath. There was only one person who could talk some sense into me.

Aarav.

*****

It took three rings before a very groggy voice answered.

"Dude, it's 3 A.M."

"I need to talk."

A beat of silence. Then a sigh.

"Where are you?"

*****

Ten minutes later, Aarav slid into the passenger seat, rubbing his eyes. He was in his sweatpants and hoodie, hair a mess as he had barely woken up before dragging himself out of bed.

"This better be life or death." He mumbled, stifling a yawn.

I let out a hollow laugh. "Feels like it."

Aarav studied me, his tiredness fading just enough to show genuine curiosity. "Okay, what's up?"

I hesitated. I had told Aarav about Anaya before—of course I did. He had known about the stupid mess of our relationship. But this? This felt different.

Still, there was no backing out now.

"I had a dream," I started, my voice quieter than usual. "About Anaya."

Aarav smirked. "Not the worst start to a story."

I shot him a look. "She was with someone else."

That wiped the smirk right off his face. "Oh."

"He was tall, good-looking, confident—the whole package. She was happy. Really happy." My grip on the steering wheel tightened. "And I—I was just standing there. Watching."

Aarav did not respond immediately. He stared at me, his gaze unreadable, as if waiting. Then, he sighed.

"Alright. Let's get this straight. You had a dream where Anaya moved on. You freaked out. And now you're here, looking like someone just stole your last meal. Kabir, what are we really talking about here?"

I looked away. "Nothing. It was just a dream."

Aarav let out a low chuckle. "No, it wasn't."

I clenched my jaw. "What do you want me to say?"

"The truth." Aarav's tone softened, but his words were sharp. "That maybe you aren't as clueless as you pretend to be. Maybe you know exactly what you feel for Anaya, but you are just too damn scared to say it."

My breath hitched because Aarav was right. But admitting it? That was a different battle altogether.

Aarav leaned back, crossing his arms. "You know, I get it. You've spent so long treating her like a good friend that changing that feels terrifying. But tell me one thing, Kabir."

I swallowed. "What?"

"If the dream was real—if she actually did find someone else—could you live with that?"

Silence. A heavy, suffocating silence.

19

Kabir

Aarav's question echoed in my head, refusing to fade. My throat felt dry, and for a long moment, I had nothing to say. Because the answer - the real, undeniable truth - was that even the thought of that dream coming true was scaring me.

I wanted Anaya to be happy. Of course, I did. But I couldn't stand the idea of her being happy with someone else.

I had avoided this for too long, hiding behind uncertainty, but that needed to change. If I wanted to be in Anaya's life the way I truly wanted, I had to stop hesitating. I had to be the man she deserved - someone who was sure of his feelings and wouldn't let her slip away because of fear.

I exhaled sharply, my grip on the steering wheel loosening. Then, finally, I looked at Aarav.

He raised an eyebrow, waiting for me to say something. I could tell he noticed the shift in my expression, the way my shoulders straightened, the hesitation finally melting away.

"Well," he said, stretching his legs out, "took you long enough."

I let out a dry chuckle, shaking my head. "You're really enjoying this, aren't you?"

"Oh, absolutely," he grinned. "Watching you lose your mind over your friend? Best entertainment I've had in a while."

I rolled my eyes but didn't argue. Because for the first time, I wasn't running from the truth.

Whatever I felt for Anaya... it wasn't something I could ignore anymore. Maybe I hadn't always seen it clearly, maybe it had crept on me when I wasn't paying attention - but now? Now it was undeniable.

"So, what now?" Aarav asked, watching me carefully. "You gonna sit around and hope she reads your mind, or are you actually going to do something about it?"

I sighed, leaning back in my seat. "I don't know. She asked me if I led her on, and I couldn't even give her a proper answer."

Aarav scoffed. "That's because you're an idiot."

"Thanks for the support."

"Anytime," he smirked. "But seriously, Kabir. You need to tell her before it is too late."

His words hit harder than I expected. Because if my dream had taught me anything, I could lose her. And if that happened, it would be nobody's fault but mine.

I rubbed my temple. "It's not that simple."

"Of course it is," Aarav shot back. "You tell her the truth. You tell her you've been an idiot. You tell her you want her - not as a friend, not as a maybe, but as someone you know you can't lose."

I swallowed. "And what if I've already messed up?"

Aarav stared at me for a moment before shaking his head. "You haven't." His voice softened, losing its usual teasing edge. "Not yet. But if you keep waiting and let your fear win, you will."

A weight settled in my chest, but this time, it was not fear; it was determination. I had spent too long being unsure, too long second-guessing every step. It was time to do something about it.

I let out a slow breath, gripping the steering wheel. "I need to fix this," I muttered.

Aarav leaned back, arms crossed. "And how exactly do you plan on doing that? She's in Hyderabad, remember?"

Reality hit me like a brick. I couldn't just show up at her doorstep. I couldn't fix this in one grand moment of clarity. She was miles away, and all I had was a phone and a lot of damage control to do.

Frustration was bubbling up inside me. "I don't know. I can't just call her up and say, 'Hey, so I might be in love with you. My bad for taking forever to figure it out.'"

Aarav snorted, "It's not the worst idea."

I shot him a glare.

He smirked. "But seriously, you don't have to figure it all out in one night. Just… stop running and start being honest with yourself first."

I nodded. "Okay. No more dodging. No more confusion. I just-" I hesitated, fingers tapping against the steering wheel. "I need to talk to her. But I don't want to rush this. I need to do it right."

Aarav clapped a hand on my shoulder. "Then do it right. But don't take too long, or you'll be calling me to cry about her wedding invitation."

I groaned. "Dude."

He laughed. "Just saying."

I shook my head, but I knew he was right deep down.

I didn't have a perfect plan, and I didn't have all the answers, but I wasn't afraid to admit what I wanted. I was done wasting time.

20

Anaya

It had been a week since our last call. A week since I told myself I wouldn't be the one to reach out first.

At first, it was easy. I kept myself busy with work and late-night conversations with Zoya that drifted from gossip to deep existential debates. But no matter what I did, there was always a moment, a pause in my day, when my mind circled back to him—to Kabir.

Had he thought about calling me? Or had that conversation been another passing moment for him, one he didn't dwell on the way I did?

I sighed, stirring my coffee absentmindedly as I sat by the window of a quiet cafe near my office. Zoya was sitting across the table, scrolling through reels.

The coffee shop smelled like freshly ground beans, warm cinnamon, and something sweet I couldn't quite place. I inhaled deeply, letting the scent wrap around me like a blanket.

But then, for a second- there was something else.

A different scent. His scent.

I stiffened.

It was faint, barely there, but unmistakable. The sharp yet smooth perfume I had grown so used to over the years, the one lingering in his car, in his clothes, in every memory I had of him.

I instinctively turned my head, scanning the cafe like I expected him to be standing there. Of course, he wasn't.

I clenched my fingers around my coffee cup, swallowing the lump in my throat. It's just someone else wearing the same fragrance, Anaya. Don't be ridiculous.

But it was too late. The scent had already done its job.

I was back in his car, windows rolled down, the city lights flickering past us. His fingers drummed against the steering wheel, the low hum of music playing in the background. That night- the hug, the hesitation, the way my heart pounded against my ribs. His arms that had stayed around me for a second too long.

I squeezed my eyes shut. Why am I thinking about this now?

"Anaya?" Zoya's voice snapped me out of it.

I looked up to find her looking at me curiously. "You okay? You spaced out for a second."

I forced a smile. "Yeah. Just……thought of something."

Her gaze sharpened immediately. "Kabir?"

"I hate how predictable I am." I sighed.

She smirked, resting her chin on her hand. "You're not predictable. You're just…obvious."

I groaned, stirring my coffee unnecessarily. "I wasn't even thinking about it until this stupid perfume!"

Zoya raised a brow. "His perfume?"

I nodded, exasperated. "Some guy is wearing the same one, and now my brain has decided to torture me."

She hummed in amusement. "Scent is the strongest trigger for memory, you know? One whiff and the past isn't just remembered, it's relived."

"Great. Love that for me."

Zoya tilted her head. "So……what exactly came to your mind?"

I hesitated. "That night. The hug. The way he…. didn't pull away."

"And?"

"And I don't know." I admitted. "I don't know what it meant. I don't know what he's thinking. I don't know if I should wait for him to say something."

Zoya studied me for a moment before leaning back. "Do you want to wait?"

That was the real question. Wasn't it?

I had spent so many years wanting Kabir that not waiting for him felt foreign. I felt like I wouldn't even know what to do with myself if I stopped hoping.

But how long could I keep holding onto something uncertain?

I exhaled slowly, looking down at my coffee. "I don't know."

Zoya reached over and squeezed my hand. "Then maybe it's time to figure it out."

I nodded, but the truth is, I didn't even know where to start.

21

Kabir

It had been a week since I spoke to Anaya. A week since I decided I wouldn't run from this anymore. And yet I hadn't called. Hadn't texted. Hadn't done anything to close the distance between us. But not because I was hesitating. Because I wanted to do this right.

Anaya wasn't just someone I could call up on a whim and confess my feelings to over a weak, half-hearted conversation. She deserved more than that. She deserved clarity and effort - she deserved to know that I wasn't just waking up one day and realising I had feelings for her. That this wasn't some fleeting impulse.

I had lost so much time to my confusion. I wouldn't let that happen again. So, I planned.

Every night, I lay awake in bed, thinking about how to do it. Should I just show up at her doorstep? No, that would feel too sudden, too overwhelming. Should I send something first? A letter? A gift? But what would that even say?

I miss you. I should have done it sooner. I'm here now.

It sounded right, but it wasn't enough.

By the fourth night, Aarav caught on.

"You're not sleeping," he pointed out as we sat on my balcony, a cool breeze running through the silence between us.

"I'm fine," I muttered.

Aarav snorted. "Sure. That's why you're staring at your phone like it holds the meaning of life."

I exhaled sharply. "I'm trying to figure out how to see her."

That made him pause. "You mean......you're actually going to Hyderabad?"

I nodded.

His brows shot up. "Okay, didn't expect you to grow a spine this fast."

I rolled my eyes. "I just can't let her keep wondering what I feel. And I need to see her face when I tell her. I need to know if there's still a chance."

Aarav leaned back, studying me. "And what's the plan? You just gonna knock on her door and declare your undying love?"

"Not exactly. I don't want her to feel cornered. I need to do this in a way that lets her decide if she wants to hear me out."

Aarav hummed in thought. "What does Anaya like? What would make her listen instead of slamming the door in your face?"

That was the question. What did Anaya love enough that it would make her pause?

Then it hit me.

Books.

She had always loved bookstores. The smell of pages, the quiet comfort of getting lost in a world that wasn't her own.

If I could just get her to meet me there - not force her, not overwhelm her, but just...in a space that felt familiar to her - it would be enough.

I reached for my phone and searched for bookstores in Hyderabad. After scrolling through a dozen, I found one that felt right—a small, cosy place near her office—the kind of place she'd visit.

I booked my tickets that night.

Aarav watched me with a smirk. "You're really doing this."

I met his gaze, my voice steady. "Yeah. I am."

He nodded approvingly. "About time."

But a thought gnawed at me as I lay in bed later, staring at my flight confirmation.

She might not come. She might not want to see me.

But that fear didn't stop me because I would rather fight for her and lose than never try.

22

Kabir

———◆◆———

The flight to Hyderabad felt like the longest journey of my life. My mind kept circling back the whole time to the same thought: What if she doesn't show up?

I had spent the past week planning this—choosing the right place, making sure it wasn't overwhelming, and making sure she had the choice to come or not. But that was the problem. She had the choice, and I had no idea what she would choose.

By the time I stepped out of the airport, Hyderabad's evening air wrapped around me - warmer than I expected, carrying the distant scent of rain-soaked roads. It felt different from home.

I hailed a cab, giving the driver the address of my hotel. The ride was silent, the city blurring past me in streaks of headlights and neon signs.

I tried not to wonder what she was doing at that very moment if she was out with Zoya. If she had any idea I was here.

Once I checked in, I set my bag down and pulled out my phone. I didn't have Zoya's number. Never needed it before. But now, she was the only person who could help me.

So I did something I never thought I'd do - I sent her a follow request on Instagram.

It took her less than a minute to accept it. Before I could overthink it, I sent a message.

Me: Hey. I need your help.

Her reply came almost instantly.

Zoya: Oh? The man finally shows up.

I sighed. I should've expected that.

Me: Not here to argue. I just... I need Anaya to be at a bookstore tomorrow. The one near her office - The Reading Nook. Can you get her there after work?

There was a long pause before she responded.

Zoya: You sure about this, Kabir?

Me: More than I've ever been.

Another pause. Then -

Zoya: Fine. But don't mess this up.

I let out a breath I didn't know I was holding.

Tomorrow.

Tomorrow, I will see her. And for the first time, I would tell her exactly what she meant to me.

No more hesitation. No more running.

Just us.

And whatever happened next.

23

Anaya

I should have known something was off. Zoya had been acting strangely the entire evening - too eager, too insistent that we stop by the bookstore before heading home. I had been reluctant, exhausted from a long day at work, but she had practically dragged me inside.

"Just five minutes," she said, grinning mischievously. "I saw this new book series you'd love."

I sighed, running my fingers along the spines of the books absentmindedly. The warm scent of paper and ink wrapped around me, familiar and comforting. Zoya had wandered off, leaving me in the fiction aisle.

And then I felt it. A shift in the air. The unshakeable feeling of being watched.

My fingers stilled over the book I was pretending to be interested in, my breath suddenly uneasy. I turned my head slowly, as if drawn by an invisible force.

And I saw him.

Kabir.

Standing a few feet away, watching me.

For a second, I thought my mind was playing tricks on me. Maybe I imagined him the same way my thoughts conjured him in quiet moments of the day. But no - he was real. Right here.

My stomach dropped. Why? Why was he here in Hyderabad? In the bookstore?

The last time we had spoken had been over a week ago. A conversation that left me confused, unsure, waiting. But he hadn't called. He hadn't texted. And now, here he was, in front of me, like the universe had decided to stop playing fair.

I swallowed hard. My heart was racing, my mind scrambling for something - anything - to say.

But before I could even open my mouth, he moved.

*****

Kabir

I had imagined this moment a hundred times. I had planned every word, rehearsed the perfect way to explain myself, to make her understand why it had taken so long. But standing here, watching the way Anaya's eyes widened in shock, how her fingers curled slightly against the book she was holding - every thought slipped from my mind.

She was here. Right in front of me.

I had spent a week trying to make this happen, convincing myself that showing up was the right thing to do. I wanted to fix things; I had to be here, not just a voice on the phone or a message on her screen.

But now that I was here, I had no idea how to start.

So I did the only thing I could. I took a step towards her.

"Hi," I said, my voice quieter than I intended.

Anaya blinked like she was still trying to process the fact that I was real.

"Hi," she said back, hesitant.

A beat of silence stretched between us, filled with words we hadn't said, with all the unanswered questions lingering between us.

Then, softly, she asked, "What are you doing here, Kabir?"

I exhaled slowly. I could lie. I could come up with some excuse, pretend I was here for work, for anything other than her.

But I was done pretending.

"I came here to see you," I admitted, watching her reaction slowly.

She sucked in a breath, her fingers tightening around the book in her hand. "Why?"

I swallowed. "Because I finally figured it out."

Her lips parted slightly, but no words came out.

I took another step closer.

"I couldn't stop thinking about you," my voice was low but certain. "And I got tired of running from it."

Her throat bobbed, emotions flickering across her face so quickly I couldn't catch them all. Shock. Confusion. Something else.

But I wasn't scared of what would happen next because I wouldn't let her slip away. Not this time.

24

Anaya

It felt like the air had been knocked out of my lungs. I stared at him, my grip tightening around the book in my hands.

You just can't say that, Kabir.

Not after all this time. Not after I had spent a week convincing myself to move on, telling myself that waiting for him was pointless. And definitely not after he had spent years treating me like I was just his friend.

Yet, here he was. In Hyderabad. Standing in front of me in a bookstore, saying he couldn't stop thinking about me.

A part of me wanted to close the book, put it back on the shelf, and pretend this wasn't happening. That I wasn't feeling everything I had spent years to suppress.

But another part of me - the one that still ached from all the uncertainty, the one that had spent nights overthinking about every little thing he ever said - refused to stay quiet.

"You can't just say that," I whispered.

Kabir exhaled, rubbing the back of his neck. "Why not?"

Why not? Why not?

I clenched my jaw, shaking my head. "Because it's not fair."

His brows pulled together. "Anaya-"

"No," I stepped back, putting distance between us. If I let him stand close, I would forget why I was upset. "You never-" My voice wavered, but I forced myself to continue. "You never said anything before. You never made me think I could......expect this from you."

His expression twisted with something that looked a lot like regret.

"I know," he admitted, his voice rough. "I know I messed up. I know I should have said something sooner. But I-" He stopped, inhaling sharply. "I was scared."

I let out a dry laugh, bitterness creeping into my tone. "Scared of what?"

"Of losing you," he said simply.

I sucked in a breath.

He took a step closer. "I thought if I ignored it and buried it deep enough, I could keep things as they were. I wouldn't have to risk ruining everything. But then you asked me if I led you on, and then, for the first time, I realised if I kept waiting, I might actually lose you anyway."

His words dug into every fragile piece of me, unearthing things I wasn't ready to feel.

"Then why didn't you say something sooner?" I asked, voice barely above a whisper.

His eyes searched mine. "Because I wanted to do this right."

Right.

I swallowed. "And you think showing up here and saying all this is the right way?"

He hesitated. "I think it's the only way."

A shaky breath left my lips. It felt like I was standing on the edge of something, not knowing whether to step forward or back away.

But could I trust him?

Silence stretched between us, the weight of everything unspoken pressing down on me.

Kabir reached for my hand, his fingers curling around mine in a way that felt too familiar, too easy - like muscle memory.

"Please," he said softly.

And just like that, I was sixteen again, my heart racing at how he spoke to me.

I had spent so many years waiting for this moment. But now that it was here, I didn't know what to do with it.

25

Kabir

I had played this moment over and over in my head how I would say it. How she would react. How, maybe, she would let me fix this.

But nothing could have prepared me for how she looked at me. She didn't know whether to believe me or run away in the opposite direction.

And honestly? I didn't blame her. She had spent years waiting for me to see her, to give her a reason for hope. And instead, all I had ever given her was silence.

When I was finally here, laying everything in front of her, she didn't know what to do with this.

I did this. I was the reason she was hesitating, the reason she didn't trust my words. And that realisation hit harder than I expected.

She didn't pull her hand away, but she didn't squeeze it either. She just stood there, staring at me, as if trying to decide whether it was real.

Whether I was real.

"Anaya," I said softly, trying to anchor her back to me, to us.

Her lips parted, but no words came out.

I took a slow breath, forcing myself to stay steady. "I know I don't deserve you to believe me immediately. I know I've spent too long being an idiot about this. But I swear to you, Anaya - I'm not here to confuse you. I'm not here to make you wait anymore."

Her eyes flickered with something unreadable. "Then why are you here?"

I swallowed, the weight of the moment pressing against my ribs.

"Because I love you."

Her breath hitched.

"I don't know when it happened," I admitted. "Maybe it was always there, and I was just too blind to see it. But I know now. And I'm not going to let fear or hesitation stop me from telling you."

Her fingers twitched in my grasp.

I held on, not too tight, just enough for her to know I meant every word.

"I came here because I wanted to prove it to you," I continued, voice quieter now. "That you're not someone I can let go of. That you're not just a maybe to me anymore."

Silence.

Anaya looked at me like she was trying to find something, some proof that I wasn't just saying this because I was afraid of losing her. That it wasn't guilt or impulsiveness or some misplaced sense of obligation.

She was searching for certainty. So, I gave it to her.

I gently lifted her hand, pressing it against my chest, right where my heart was pounding against my ribs. "It's yours," I said, barely above a whisper. "It always has been. I just didn't realise it in time."

Her eyes snapped up to mine, wide, vulnerable.

My pulse was a mess.

This was it. The moment that could change everything.

She could say she didn't trust me, that I was too late, or that she had moved on, and I would have to live with that.

But she didn't say anything. She just stood there, her palm resting against my heart, feeling every unspoken word beneath it.

And for the first time in my life, I realised-

Some things are worth waiting for.

Even if they take forever.

Even if they terrify you.

Even if the person you love isn't sure whether to let you in again.

I would wait.

For her, I would wait.

26

Anaya

———✦✦———

I wanted Kabir for so long. And now, I could finally have him.

If sixteen-year-old me could see this moment, she would've screamed, jumped around in excitement, probably run in circles before collapsing in her bed in disbelief.

She had spent years wishing for this.

He was the boy I imagined every time I listened to a love song, the one I thought of while watching a romantic movie. The one I had spent too long hoping would see me the way I saw him.

And now - he did.

The weight of his confession was still settling in my chest, but nothing hit harder than the way his heart pounded against my palm.

Fast. Unsteady. Almost frantic.

And when he whispered,

It's yours. It always has been

Something inside me cracked wide open. It wasn't just his words. It was how he said them.

Like they had been trapped inside him for years, waiting to be let out. He had spent too long pretending they weren't real, only to realise he couldn't hold them back anymore.

It wasn't a last-minute realisation born out of fear.

This was him. Kabir. Finally, standing in front of me, not just as my friend, not as a boy figuring things out - but as a man who knew exactly what he wanted.

And maybe I should've been careful. Maybe I should've asked more questions, made him prove it, and tested his certainty's depth.

But I didn't. Because the truth was - I believed him.

Maybe it was stupid. Maybe it was reckless. But I knew what it felt like to be unsure. I had spent years feeling that way, constantly questioning where I stood with him, wondering if I was just reading too much into things.

But this?

This wasn't uncertainty.

This was **Kabir in love with me.**

And I wouldn't waste another second pretending I didn't want this.

I let out a slow breath, my fingers curling slightly against his chest. I felt the wild rhythm of his heartbeat beneath my touch.

He watched me carefully, waiting for me to say something, his entire body tense - like he was bracing himself for the worst.

Like he was afraid, I was going to walk away.

I didn't.

Instead, I smiled. Just a little. Just enough for him to see I wasn't running.

His breath hitched.

I tilted my head, voice barely above a whisper. "Kabir."

He swallowed, his grip on my hand tightening just slightly. "Hmm?"

I could've said a hundred things at that moment.

That I forgave him.

That I had spent too many years waiting to doubt him now.

But in the end, I just said that one thing mattered the most.

"I love you too."

The tension in his body disappeared in an instant, as if he had been holding onto a breath for years and had finally let it go.

And then - he smiled.

Not a smirk, not the teasing grin I had seen a thousand times.

A *real* smile. One that reached his eyes, lighting up every part of his face like he couldn't believe this was happening.

And just like that, sixteen-year-old Anaya finally got what she had been waiting for all along.

27

Anaya

The air between us felt different now. Lighter, yet heavier in ways I couldn't describe. We had just stepped into something uncharted—something we had both secretly wanted but never dared to touch until now.

Kabir was holding my face, his thumb grazing my cheek as if memorising my feel. His heartbeat had slowed a little, but I could still feel the echoes of it beneath my fingertips. Rapid. Reckless. Like mine.

I let out a breath. "So… this is real?"

His lips quirked up, but his eyes held something softer, something that made my own heart trip over itself. "It is. If you want it to be."

I swallowed, nodding. I did. I so did.

I closed my eyes briefly, pressing my forehead against his chest, breathing him in. He wrapped his arms around me, pulling me closer, as if he had been waiting for so long to do this.

"Anaya," he murmured against my hair, his voice almost hesitant.

"Yeah?"

He pulled back slightly, just enough to look at me. "Go out with me tomorrow."

I blinked. "What?"

"A date." His lips curled into a smile. "A real one. No weird tension, no pretending. Just us. After work, I'll pick you up."

I stared at him, feeling something warm bloom in my chest. "You're serious?"

He chuckled. "Anaya. I've never been more serious."

A slow, delighted grin spread across my face. "Okay."

His smile widened, and before I could overthink it, he dipped his head and kissed my forehead softly. "Good."

*****

The moment I entered the apartment, Zoya was already grinning like she had won the lottery.

"Well?" She demanded, practically vibrating with excitement. "How did it go?"

I set my bag down, looking at her with a smile. "Kabir asked me out."

She let out a loud gasp before dramatically flopping onto the couch. "Oh my God. I knew it. I knew this day would come, but it still feels like some crazy climax." She sat up suddenly, her eyes wide. "How did he do it? Was it cute? Did you cry? Did he cry?"

I rolled my eyes, kicking off my shoes. "No one cried."

"That's disappointing." She muttered, but her grin stayed intact. "Okay, fine, details! What did he say? How did you react? Tell me everything."

I sat beside her, hugging a cushion against my chest. "It wasn't anything grand. He just asked me like it was the most natural thing in the world."

She squealed, grabbing my arm. "Because it *is* the most natural thing in the world! You guys are *finally* happening." She shook her head in disbelief.

I laughed. "It feels weird, you know? I've wanted this for so long but now that it's real, it feels overwhelming."

"It's not weird. It's just… finally happening. And you deserve it."

I swallowed.

Tomorrow, I will be on a date with Kabir. Not as a friend, not as someone waiting on the sidelines. But as someone he had finally chosen. And I wasn't afraid to believe it.

28

Kabir

I checked my watch for the fifth time in the last two minutes. She'd be out any second now. My heart was beating way too fast. Tonight was different.

Tonight, I wasn't just her friend. I was the guy who was taking her on a date.

I glanced down at the bouquet in my hands. Simple, elegant. Not too over the top, but thoughtful. I had spent an embarrassing amount of time at the florist's trying to decide which flowers to get. Roses felt too cliché. Lilies were nice, but I wasn't sure if she liked them. So, I settled on a mix - soft pastel shades, delicate yet vibrant. Just like her. I had also rented a car, knowing how much Anaya loves drives.

The moment the glass doors swung open, I straightened, my fingers tightening around the bouquet.

And then I saw her.

She stepped out, scanning the road, looking for me. The streetlights cast a soft glow around her, and for a second, I just stood there, taking her in. She looked beautiful - not in the way that made you stop and stare - but in the way that made you feel.

I took a deep breath and stepped forward, my voice steady despite the way my pulse raced.

"Waiting for someone?"

Anaya's gaze flickered to me, and for a brief second, surprise flashed across her face before it melted into something softer. Her eyes dropped to the bouquet in my hand.

"You brought me flowers?"

I shrugged, trying to play it cool. "Well, yeah. Thought I'd make a good first impression."

She let out a quiet laugh, shaking her head. "Kabir, you don't need flowers to impress me."

"I know." I took a step closer, holding out the bouquet. "But I wanted to."

She looked at me then, really looked at me, as if seeing something she hadn't seen before. Slowly, she reached out and took the flowers from my hands.

"They're beautiful," she murmured.

"So are you."

Her eyes snapped up to mine, and for a moment, neither of us spoke.

And then she smiled. The kind that made my chest too small for my heart.

"Come on," I said, nodding towards the car. "Let's get out of here."

She nodded, still holding the flowers close, and followed me into the car. As we got into the car, I realised something.

This was it. This was the start of us.

29

Anaya

The car ride was quiet, but not uncomfortable. It was the kind of silence that felt full-charged with unspoken things, stolen glances, and the warmth of knowing we were exactly where we were meant to be.

I held the bouquet in my lap, tracing the petals absently, stealing a look at Kabir as he drove. His hands gripped the wheel with quiet confidence; his sleeves rolled up just enough to reveal his forearms. The faint hum of the car's engine mixed with the distant sounds of the city, and for a moment, it felt like we were in our own little world.

And then, we reached the cafe.

Kabir parked the car and stepped out, walking over to my side even before I could reach for the door handle.

When I looked up, he was already there, opening the door for me, his eyes holding a warmth that made my heart stutter.

There he stood.

Six feet of perfection.

My six feet of perfection.

I swallowed, stepping out slowly, my fingers brushing past his as he closed the door behind me. The warmth of his touch lingered, spreading through me like a quiet ache.

He tilted his head slightly, watching me. "What?"

I shook my head, smiling. "Nothing."

*****

The cafe was exactly the kind of place I loved-small, warm, and tucked away from the chaos of the city. String lights hung from the ceiling, casting a golden glow over the wooden tables. A soft melody played in the background, the kind that made you want to slow down and savour every moment.

Kabir pulled out my chair before taking the seat across from me, and I couldn't help but smile. "Look at you, being all gentlemanly."

He leaned forward, resting his elbows on the table. "I've always been a gentleman. You're just noticing now?"

I rolled my eyes, but the butterflies in my stomach refused to settle.

A waiter came by and Kabir let me order before placing his own. The moment we were alone again, he exhaled, drumming his fingers against the table.

"I have a confession," he said.

"Oh?" I raised a brow.

He leaned back, looking almost sheepish. "I was overthinking this entire date the whole week. I planned, cancelled, and replanned. And even now, sitting with you, I still can't believe this is real."

"Kabir……"

He shook his head, his gaze locking onto mine. "No, really. I spent too long being an idiot about my feelings for you. And now when I finally do this right, I don't want to mess up."

I swallowed past the lump in my throat. "You're not messing it up."

Kabir's shoulders relaxed slightly, and his lips curved into that small, heart-stopping smile.

The food arrived, but I barely tasted it. Every moment felt like it was suspended in time: the way his fingers brushed against mine when he passed me the salt, the way he listened to me like it was the most important thing in the world, and then there was the way he looked at me, like I was the only thing that mattered.

I had spent so many years imagining this exact moment. And now that I finally had it, it felt even better than I could've ever dreamed.

I smiled to myself, shaking my head slightly.

"What?" Kabir asked.

I looked at him, heart full. "Nothing. Just happy."

His gaze softened, and without a word, he reached across the table, lacing his fingers into mine. And just like that, the world outside ceased to exist.

30

Anaya

—◆◆—

The drive back was filled with laughter, stolen glances, and the kind of warmth that settled deep in my chest. For once, I wasn't overthinking. I wasn't waiting for something to go wrong.

Kabir was here. With me. And this time he wasn't running.

When we reached my apartment, he parked but didn't move to turn off the engine. Instead, he exhaled slowly, resting his hands on the wheel before finally turning to face me.

"So how does long distance work?" His voice was light, teasing. "Do I send you good morning texts or handwritten letters? Actually, no - scratch that. My handwriting is a masterpiece. You'd frame my letters."

I laughed, shaking my head. "You really think highly of yourself, huh?"

His laughter faded into something quieter, something softer. He reached over, tucking a strand of hair behind my ear.

"I mean it, though." He said, his thumb grazing my cheek. "I don't want distance to change anything. I don't want us to go back to almost."

I held his gaze, my heart pounding. "We won't. You're stuck with me now."

His lips parted like he wanted to say something, but instead, he leaned in.

Slowly.

Giving me every chance to move away. But I didn't.

His hand cupped my face, his warmth seeping into my skin, and then -

His lips met mine.

It wasn't hesitant. It wasn't unsure. It was everything we held back for years, Everything we had never said out loud.

I reached him, my fingers curling into his shirt as he pulled me impossibly closer.

When we finally broke apart, my breath was uneven, my skin tingling. He rested his forehead against mine, his lips curving into a smile.

"That's one way to say goodbye," he murmured.

I traced my fingers along his jaw, smiling. "Not goodbye. Just a small pause."

"Then I can't wait to hit play again."

*****

The next morning, I dropped him off at the airport, there were no heavy goodbyes, no unspoken words. Just a promise.

He pulled me into a tight hug. "I'll be back even before you have time to miss me."

I smirked. "Oh? So, by tomorrow?"

He chuckled. "I knew you'd miss me first."

I rolled my eyes but held onto him just for a second longer.

As he walked towards the entrance, he turned back one last time. "Don't fall in love with someone else."

I crossed my arms. "Bit late for that. Don't you think?"

His smile softened. "Yeah. It is."

And then he was gone.

But I wasn't left wondering. Because no matter how many miles stretched between us, I knew one thing for sure-

Kabir was mine. And I was his.